Laura kerr

Text copyright © Sally Grindley 1998
Illustrations copyright © Tania Hurt-Newton 1998

First published in Great Britain in 1998
by Macdonald Young Books
an imprint of Wayland Publishers Ltd
61 Western Road
Hove
East Sussex
BN3 1JD

Find Macdonald Young Books on the internet at http://www.myb.co.uk

Printed in Hong Kong by Wing King Tong.

British Library Cataloguing in Publication Data available

ISBN 0 7500 2543 3

SALLY GRINDLEY

MULBERRY
alone in the park

Illustrated by Tania Hurt-Newton

MACDONALD YOUNG BOOKS

The front door had been left open.
Mulberry stood in the hall and looked
puzzled.
"Is it doggy walkies time?" he barked.
"It doesn't feel like doggy walkies time
but I'm happy to go."

Nobody came.
"We could go to the park," he barked.
Still nobody came. "Then I'll go on my own," barked Mulberry.

He trotted down the steps before he could change his mind. At the bottom, he looked right and then left and then right again and went left.

Soon he came to a road.
Cars zoomed past him – zoom!
Lorries boomed past him – boom!
Mulberry didn't like it. They were too
fast and too loud.

Mulberry saw a gap. Run for it, Mulberry, run! He stepped off the pavement. Toot toot toot! Honk honk honk! Screeeeech! Mulberry didn't like cross voices so he kept on running.

At last he reached the park. He raced over to the trees. A squirrel ran across the grass. It stopped and stared at Mulberry.
Mulberry stared back.
"You run and I'll chase you," growled Mulberry.

Time to chase squirrels!

The squirrel
ran up a tree.
"You were too
quick," barked
Mulberry. The squirrel
jumped across to another
tree. "Come back down,"
barked Mulberry. The squirrel
jumped across to another tree and
another until it was out of sight.

11

Mulberry pretended not to care.
He ran through the fallen leaves,
grabbed a stick in his jaws and trotted
along a path.

Another dog came trotting along the
path towards him. Mulberry stopped
and growled. The other dog snarled.

The other dog ran at Mulberry.
Mulberry tried to escape. The other
dog was fast. Mulberry could feel him
catching up. Mulberry could feel his
hot dog breath.

Then somebody shouted cross words.
"Stop it, Tugger, stop! Come to heel
now!" Mulberry stopped and looked
round. Tugger went to heel.

He turned to stare at Mulberry.
Mulberry wagged his tail and trotted
away with the stick still in his jaws.

The path led to the pond. There were ducks round the pond. Mulberry leapt into the water – splash! Quack quack quack! quacked the ducks. They flapped their wings and paddled away from him.

Mulberry doggy-paddled as fast as he
could.
"Wait for me," he gasped.
Quack quack quack! quacked the
ducks. They flapped their wings and
flew away.

Mulberry saw a little boat sailing towards him. He doggy-paddled over to it and grabbed it in his jaws.

A boy shouted at him. Mulberry jumped out of the water and ran over to him.

He dropped the boat on the ground
and shook the water from his fur.
"Time for my pat on the head," he
barked. "Bad dog!" shouted the boy.
Mulberry pricked up his ears.
"Bad dog! Naughty dog!"

Mulberry looked puzzled.
"You've broken my boat!" shouted
the boy.

Mulberry's ears dropped. "Did I do wrong?" he whimpered. He walked away with his tail between his legs.

He settled down under a bush and was soon fast asleep.

Mulberry was woken by a bang!
And another – bang!
And then another – bang!

He howled with fright and shot out
from underneath the bush. It was dark.
Mulberry had never been in the park in
the dark.

Suddenly something pink and green
and orange shot up into the sky and lit
up the park. Bang! Bang! Bang!
Mulberry ran howling along the path.

"I want to go home," he barked. Bang!

"I want my doggy basket." Bang!

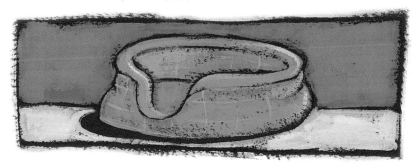

"I want my chewy bone and I want my squeaky ball." Bang! Bang! Bang!

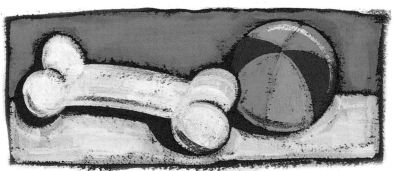

The path was blocked. There were legs everywhere. Something gold and silver screeched into the sky and exploded in a shower of stars. Mulberry yelped with fear as they fell around him.

He ran through the forest of legs.
He heard shouts and screams.
People trod on his paws.

Mulberry ran as fast as he could. He saw a gate. He ran through it and out of the park.

He came to a road. Cars zoomed past him. Lorries boomed past him. Then…

"Mulberry, stay!"
Mulberry stepped off the pavement.
"Stay, Mulberry, stay!"

Mulberry pricked up an ear.
He knew that voice.

"We're coming, Mulberry. Good boy,
Mulberry, we're coming."
And there they were, full of hugs and
kind words. Mulberry leapt at them.
"I'm so pleased to see you," he barked.

"I've been so frightened. Please put on
my lead and take me home."

When he saw home, he raced to the door.

He went inside and made quite sure that the door was closed behind him.

He ate his doggy crunchy things and played with his squeaky ball.
"I'll never go to the park alone again," he whimpered as he sat in his basket.
Then he licked his paws clean, closed his eyes, and fell fast asleep.

Look out for more fun titles in the First Storybook series.

Mulberry Home Alone *by Sally Grindley*

Mulberry the dog doesn't like being home alone. But he tries to make the best of it. First he searches for his doggy crunchy things. Whoops! He's knocked over the rubbish bin. Then he decides to chase Cat. Whoops! He's crashed into the telephone table. Luckily, Mulberry isn't home alone for long.

Leon's Fancy Dress Day *by Alan MacDonald*

Leon doesn't know what to wear to the fancy dress parade. All his friends have picked the best ideas. Then he finds a black mask in his toy box. He decides to go as a big bad robber. But nobody is very scared and Leon can't see where he's going. How is he ever going to win a prize?

Leon Gets A Scarecut *by Alan MacDonald*

Leon must get his mane cut for Patsy's party. On the way to Sid's Barber Shop he meets some friends. Strangely they are all wearing new hats. Leon is a little nervous as Sid's new electric trimmer buzzes in his ears. He closes his eyes until it's over. Then he looks in the mirror. Help! He can't go to Patsy's party with a scarecut-haircut.

All these books and many more in the Storybook series can be purchased from your local bookseller. For more information about Storybooks, write to: *The Sales Department, Macdonald Young Books, 61 Western Road, Hove, East Sussex BN3 1JD.*